Designed by Flowerpot Press
in Franklin, TN.
www.FlowerpotPress.com
Designer: Stephanie Meyers
Editor: Katrine Crow
DJS-0912-0154
ISBN: 978-1-4867-0944-1
Made in China/Fabriqué en Chine

Martin
Finds a Way

Written by T.H. Marshall

Illustrated by Katarzyna Bukiert

One fine day, with little to no fanfare, a really nice kid named Martin began a journey.

He wasn't headed anywhere special. He was just out enjoying his life, smiling and walking, when suddenly he struck upon something...

He looked to see what it was and discovered it was a *Way*. He picked it up, tucked it under his arm, and went right on smiling and walking.

It felt good to find a *Way.*

Later, Martin walked up smiling as his friend Eugene was growing frustrated. Eugene had been working on something, but it wasn't coming together.

"Something is missing," Eugene said.

Martin showed Eugene the *Way* he had found and Eugene thought it looked perfect.

"Keep it," said Martin, as he went on smiling and walking.

It felt good to share the Way.

It wasn't too long before Martin found something again. When he looked at it, he realized he had stumbled upon another *Way*.

This was a new *Way*. Martin picked it up, looked it over, tucked it under his arm, and went right on smiling and walking.

Later, Martin ran into his friend Nancy.
Nancy was upset. Nancy had lost her *Way*.
Martin showed her the new *Way* he had found.

"This is a new *Way*," Nancy said.

"Will it help you find your *Way*?" asked Martin.

"It might," said Nancy.

"Then keep it," said Martin, who went right on smiling
and walking.

It felt good to show the *Way*.

Later still, Martin met up with his pal Dave. Dave had a very different *Way*.
He wanted Martin to see the very different *Way*. They went to look at it.

"You're right," said Martin. "This is a very different *Way*."

"Would you like to explore this *Way*?" asked Dave.

"With you?" asked Martin.

"Yes, with me," said Dave.

"Then yes," Martin said.

So, Martin spent time with Dave exploring the very different *Way*.

They examined the *Way* from many perspectives. They got to know the *Way* very well. It was a great *Way*.

But eventually Martin decided to continue his journey, so he again started walking.

The longer Martin explored, the more *Ways* he found. Martin came to realize there were many different worthwhile *Ways*.

Each *Way* had its own unique characteristics, but the *Ways* were very similar as well. They were all very good *Ways*.

Some *Ways* were perfectly suited to some people.

Other *Ways* were perfectly suited to others.

There was really no right Way or wrong Way, Martin decided.

Everyone just needs to find the Way that's right for them, he thought.

For some, that was no *Way*.

The more that Martin understood that there was not
a better *Way* or a worse *Way*, the more he came to
like the idea of finding the right *Way* for him.

And so he explored many, many *Ways*...

And eventually he found it!

He found the *Way* that fit him best.

It was the *Way* that was right for him.

And he headed that *Way*.

He is still following that *Way* today...

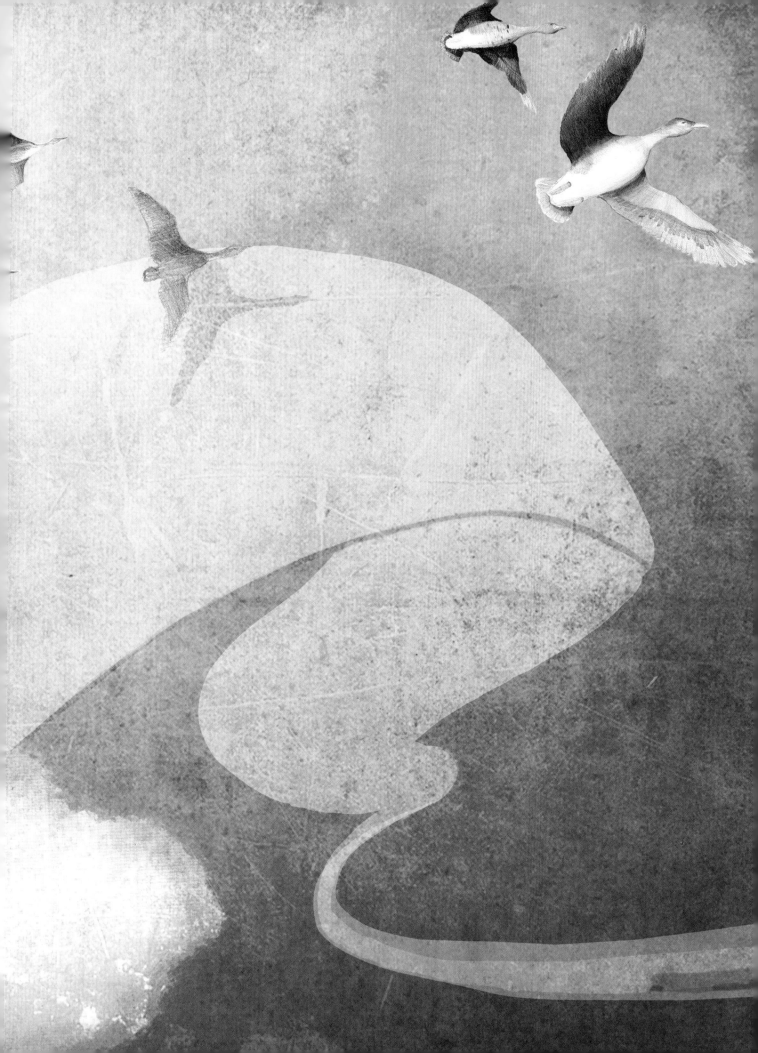

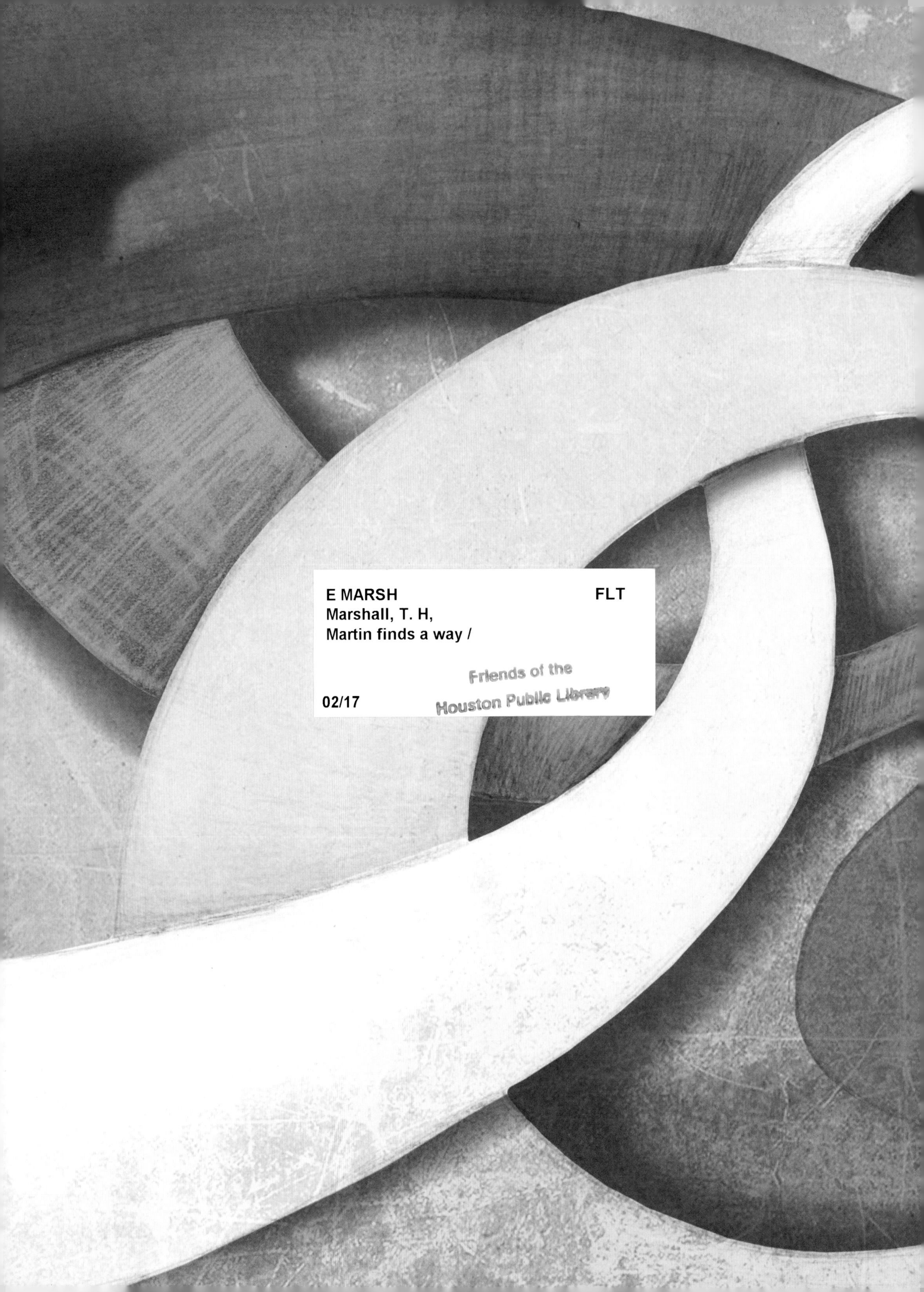